The Cat in the Grass and the Carnivorous Plant Seize the Day

B.I PHILLIPS

To order additional copies of this book, contact:
Xlibris
844-714-8691
www.Xlibris.com
Orders@Xlibris.com

ISBN: Softcover   978-1-6641-5415-5
         EBook   978-1-6641-5414-8

Print information available on the last page

Rev. date: 06/25/2021

This book belongs to : _____

The cat in the grass decides
to start the day with a swim

While swimming the carnivorous plant decides to take a hamburger off the grill where they are cooking.

The cat and carnivorous plant
decide to go to the Zoo.

They visit with giraffe who has four stomach compartments. Giraffe was served carrots .

On to next visit after giraffe.

The cat and carnivorous plant
visit with the manta rays .

More giraffes

Next they visit the Antelopes.
Carnivorous plant still has the carrot
he took from the giraffe feeding dish.

Next they visit the crab who is
having starfish being served to him.

The carnivorous plant is hungry
so he attempts to grab a starfish.

The starfish suddenly springs to life and both are knocked out.

Next they visit the Alligator

Next they visit the peacocks.

The cat says to carnivorous plant
"did you do anything
you are ashamed of today?"

Carnivorous plant returns food to the Zoo.

Printed in the United States
by Baker & Taylor Publisher Services